AT IT OF TOO TWO TUTU TO 2
IS FOR FORE (YES)∞ THE THE
THE NO AN A A OF

AT IT OF TOO TWO TUTU TO 2 IS FOR FORE (YES)∞ THE THE THE NO AN A A OF

Guy Armstrong

The Nameless Publisher

Published by Sleep-in Publishing

"We publish silly books"

Copyright 2012 by Guy Armstrong

This first edition ("beer and weed edition") published online 2012

Cover artist:
No-one, I just typed it bro!

This is my first book... I hope it enjoys you...

ISBN 978-0-473-23361-7

CONTENTS

How to Read a Book... 3

Friday Night ... 8

Recessions ... 12

The Rest of My Friday Night ... 15

Saturday Night ... 18

How to Be an Extremely Healthy Food and Fitness Guru and Get Me Rich Quick Spiritually ... 24

How to Cope with Writer's Block ... 29

INTERVENTION ... 31

How to Be the Best World in the Writer ... 35

Politics, Inventions, and UFOs ... 41

War on the Lower Class ... 45

HOW TO READ A BOOK

I was balancing a vodka, a whiskey, and a wine in one hand, three beers in the other, and was pouring some Peruvian corn port shots out along the dash. This was foolish because I needed at least two hands free to make obscene finger gestures, and another to throw empties into the yards I was driving through on my way home.

I was returning from a chairman's meeting of *The Society for Jabbing People in the Ribs with a Pencil while They're Carrying Something*, riding my tractor far beyond full volume, in second gear down the extremely steep Devon Street. It was late at night, and I was in a bad mood. I hadn't jabbed a single person in the ribs all day, and I felt much the saner for it. Bad vibes oozed off me, coating the Aro Valley hippies in worry and negativity. One of them complained; I bludgeoned him with a sackful of urinating marsupials as I drove past.

It reminded me of my great uncle Herb, who unfortunately died when he jumped into a tall building.

The next day police found me at an equality rally for ≠ signs. I'd only had eleventy-threenty-six twelvety twelve twelve seventy-five-hundredy-twelve eight eight ninety thirteenty-one beers, and I wasn't even drunk. I had six beers in my chest pocket of my T-shirt, Σ beers in my shorts, four beers tucked into my racing jandals, a doz tucked into my gym jandals, two bottles of cider hidden in a tinny, eighty-tenty-five point three beers under my bowling hat, twelve beers hidden under my batting hat and a six-pack sneakily engulfed in a rather nasty fart. "Public drinking is not tolerated, sir" they told me. "In all honesty" I lied," I have **NOT** been drinking."

Then I fell over. "I just haven't got my land legs yet." "Come on mate, what bar have you been drinking at?" they asked. "Bar Nana" I said. They scowled at me. Then they confiscated the five whiskeys I had hidden in one of my beers! To punish me for being a potential harm to myself, they beat me up. To punish me for being a potential harm to other people, they beat me down. I think because I'm a biology student, they locked me in a cell. "This is for your own good" they said. While I was inside, I was beaten up by criminals.

While I was waiting to be let out, I snacked on some dried water. "This prison food's alright" I thought. Upon release I drove round and round the Basin Reserve, I don't know how many times, in my switched reluctance bulldozer at about four miles an hour.

Then I changed vehicles. I'd kidnapped some adults a year ago in my car, so I wasn't allowed to drive that any more. In full deviant loopholing through the law, I sawed my car in half, now I have two motorbikes. But I wanted to shield myself from the Wellington wind, so I bought another car, which I promptly remembered I wasn't allowed to drive. I cut it in half lengthwise with my mate's angle grinder. It was a pretty rough cut, and I sliced some part of myself open almost every time I got in to ride.

"It's a vicious cycle" I explained to the police, who didn't seem to care, and promptly pulled me over. "No more driving round and round" they said, over and over. "I thought you guys *liked* donuts" I said. I screamed while the policewoman salted me with pepper spray. Her partner peppered me with assaults. *It's an unfair cop* I thought.

When the judge saw the axe poking out of my neck she looked me down and up. "You need to see a doctor" she told me. "Nah, yeah, true bro, I already know what a doctor looks like ay" I said. I was sentenced. Then I was paragraphed. Then I did the Billy T laugh.

As soon as I got out of jail, I was arrested for selling a massive bag of pee to a urologist. "It's not *quite* what you think" I said. The forensics department were *extremely* pissed off, about being pissed around. They had to let me off on a wee technicality. To celebrate I had a party where my band played. "Ah, can you be a bit quieter?" the airport next door said. The police turned up to turn me down. Probably because of my pioneering anti-gravity research, they said they were locking me UP.

Lawyers were expensive; I figured instead of working on a strategic defence, I would simply tell the judge it was my birthday. Surely they wouldn't jail me on my birthday! Believing in the virtue of punctuality, I was early to court. The early worm catches the dirt.

I was nervous and unprepared so I set up a kind of mental camp, to calculate all the different vectors in the courtroom. "What the hell are you doing with your life?" the judge inquired of me. I was so stressed I got my tenses, my tensors and my tents's all mixed up. "Well, tomorrow I had been hiking through cell counts with my friends. Yesterday I'm going bush for some microscopic exercise, where it's snowing." I could tell the judge was going to verbally destroy me. I lined up all my sardonic responses in a tin.

I didn't think I was making any progress trying to escape the judicial punishment system. "You'll have plenty of time for deep thinking in jail" the judge told me. "Are you sure jail's a good place for deep thinking?" I aaahst. Because of my extremely brutally epic lack of lifestyle I had two puffed up black eyes, and she didn't like the way I didn't look.

She was talking quite fast; I put my toupee on so I could hair. I had too many piercings, I took them out so I could ear. "CAN YOU FOCUS, PLEASE!" The judge shouted. It looked to some people like I wasn't looking at the facts. I squinted and strained my wonky eye, so eye could I.

I felt I owed society an explanation. "You see, your honour" I began, "I went to work sober the other day – just to see what it was like, you know? Just for something different. Turns out it was still really boring." "Don't make me pour out all this boiling rage on you" the jug said. I wished I was home, chugging back some beers and listening to Slayer on my headphones instead of being told off, for chugging back some beers and listening to Slayer on my headphones, in court. "Are you even paying attention?" accused the chug. I felt like I was a prisoner already, like one of those kids in that movie *The Breakfast Club*. "He's wasting our time, take him away" said the Judd.

They hauled me off to jail. I got thirsty almost straight away; I pulled out the bottle of whiskey I had hidden in a condom up my butt. When it came time for group showers, some really butch naked men with LOVE tattoos started winking at me. I pulled out the pack of condoms I had hidden in a condom up my butt.

"Why do I have to keep everything in my bum?" I arsed. I begged to be let out of jail. I wanted to escape. I hadn't been so depressed since my Aunt Patricia suffered a horrendous fatality when sadly, she blew her own brains out one cold winter's day, when she sneezed a little too hard.

"You're in jail for the good of society" everyone said. While I was inside, I learned how to make every drug and acquired powerful criminal connections. I finally got a lawyer, and we went to court to save me. "Why should we let you out of the circular prison cell?" The judge arcst. "Well, it all goes back to Friday night, your honour..."

2

FRIDAY NIGHT

When I thought up this joke on the way to the bank, I was laughing all the way to the bank. I put lots of money in the bank; I guess a genius and money are soon parted. I don't bank my pennies though, because I burn through them so fast I keep them in a rather large urn. I guess a penny saved is a penny urned.

I ate some gouda, it was pretty goud. Then I ate some feta, but it could have been beta. "I paté the fool who doesn't get that awesome joke" I said to the policeman who pulled me over while I was careening my forklift on half a wheel round the hairpin on Devon street over and over again after I drank thirty eleventy-five five five beers beers honey meads hundredy twelve cocaines vodka vodka ouzo CO_2 inhalation. "That's not even a joke, it should be illegal" said the balding captain while I patted him on the pate. "Surely you've got the brawn to stomach a few jokes about head cheese?" "Well it's definitely not tasting of any brain" he said.

I explained to him that while I thought up that joke, I'd just hit my head falling down a bank on the way to the bank. I often fall down, I guess a genius and altitude are soon parted. The heated friction of the fall grazed my pelvis somewhat, worse because I'd shaved my pubes that morning. I guess a pelvis shaved is a pelvis burned.

"Sir, are you indecently exposed?" I hoped I wasn't. Somehow I'd stumbled out of bed, out of breakfast, and into my pelican's mouth. I had the distinct feeling I was unpantalooned. My steed didn't mind, and we rode our way to the bank, until I fell out, somehow landing in a fork-lift I'd left there in a previous article. I always fall out of pelicans, I guess a genus and *liptornis* are soon parted.

But I'll tell you about that stuff in the past in the future. Right now, I'll tell you about just then.

"Sir are you driving under the influence?" this really blurry cop asked. My brain spun. I felt the concerns of the common man – the working-class policeman, acknowledging the detriments of our leaders, and the complicity of us in being victims. I began to say I agreed with him, there *is* a dark, malicious, sinister influence in our society, that governs with unseen hands and manipulates from behind closed doors. Was he talking about the coercive nature of advertising? The wanton destruction of our environment at the behest of a select, greedy few? I felt a bond with this law enforcer ... while we were different in employ, we were one and the same on a deeper, human level. "Are you talking about the *Illuminated Ones* and the *Secret Societies,* those roots of the tree of death we would all rise to cleave, unless us good people gradually turn into an evil race?" I orcsed. But he said no, he was talking about my drinking damnit!

I scoffed at his accusation, and his attempt to count the number of empties under the brake pedal. "Oh come on mate I've only had six-hundred and ten ten fifty-twoty-tooty-four threenty-ninety-googolty beers and I'm not even drunk" I belched.

He asked if I had a criminal record. "I've got some *Ice-T* and *Burzum* records, those dudes were criminals hardout!" I didn't want to get the wrong answer and go to jail instead of passing GO and miss out on all the student allowance nine nine nine nine billion billion dollars two hundred and something creditty debtty money.

"You students are so bloody political" the politicman said. That's weird, because I'm normally way too non-participative and paranoid to get into politics. I was too stoned on election day and forgot to vote for the dopey old ACT party, I guess a greenie and Roger Douglas are soon parted.

I told the policeman that on Friday night me and Stephen King were driving really slowly down Courtenay Place in my stealth bomber with *Holy Diver* cranking so all the boy racers would get jealous. What's the point of having a stealth bomber if you don't show it off? Then me and Jodi Picoult got in a fight with some sexual deviants on Vivian Street. It all reminded me of my great aunt Belinda, who tragically gruesomely morbidly horrifically blood-spurtingly decapitatedly died during a re-birthing workshop. Thinking of Belinda got me thinking of her husband Earl, who died when an aeroplane fell out of him.

When I got home, I received a call from the Government asking me if I had a spare ten minutes to help with an opinion survey on my experiences with the NZ legal system. I thought about it for eleven minutes, and told them I didn't. I just think it's very inappropriate, immoral and potentially quite dangerous for Big Brother to be peeking into our business all the time and know all our private little thoughts and feelings. Then I went back to reading my little brother's diary.

3

IT'S 4:20 SOMEWHERE – HOW TO COPE WITH THE RECESSION

I was just slishing my willy around in some dog turds when I heard the news: The New Zealand Government were spending a hundred billionfinity hundred sixty-eleven hundreddy-ten thousandy-million-hundreddy-positive a thousand billion million trillion Brazilian squillion dollars on a financial analysis to see if they had any spare money. When I heard about that I felt like a big jubey-lipped African woman blowing a raspberry on a baby leprechaun's tummy. Wow man, now I'm so tired I could sleep with a horse. Something something recession.

What exactly is a thingy that is meant by **BIG** words like recession?

Basically a recession is the second session of the day. Like when my flatmate Bob gets out of bed in the afternoon to play some *Fallout3*, after he's had his wake 'n' bake, coffee, and ciggy, he will go to the kitchen to put the knives back on after the first time his character is killed by a deathclaw or a Super Mutant with a spiked board. That sort of lifestyle costs money, and us students are pretty poor. So I'm glad to say that all over the world, people are helping out in the fight against poverty, or the 'war on poor'. The Americans, for instance, are sending heaps of missionaries and bibles to poor Arabs so they can go to heaven when the American army blows them to bits. The British are getting a bunch of aging rockers to stop having holidays in the French Riviera and snorting cocaine off the sculpted glutes and exquisite rosy nipples of champagne-drenched Playboy bunnies for a weekend, so their butlers can do a song about the terrible pain of poverty.

A recent generation of gamers have been destroying all of the Super Mutants in Washington DC to keep president Brak safe. And I have been sitting here having a few really wicked recessions with this new bong I made. So we are all pitching in.

Australia has told the poor people to harden the fuck up mate, which is pretty helpful. Oh yeah which reminds me! I really like that Aussie politician, Kevin Ruddy Wilson, he is FUNNY, man! I think I have one of his tapes lying around somewhere from back in the day.

And I would give the poor people one of my fifty-eleventy-six beery whiskeys, but nah, yeah, I've only got enough for myself ay.

Heaps of people in my lectures are talking about America, but America hasn't really done much in the world lately in the past 20 years. Now don't call me a racist, it's not just because they got that Maori fulla for king, it's just that other than that they've just been a bit boring, at least economically. Meanwhile, stuff in New Zealand is getting hardcore! Tinnies have gone up to *twenty-five* dollars in some parts of Wellington, and that is having a *huge* effect on the economy. No-one is letting us tick anymore! And some of my mates are saying it is better off just getting a fifty bag! But then you have to save up, it's way harder to get fifty bucks than twenty. The other day I heard some people talk about a financial recession. That is heavy, man, I hope we don't have one of them. They must have been smoking too much, though, probably just paranoid. Too much skunk. I'm sure if we just don't worry about it it'll be sweet.

I am actually testing this out as a scientific hypothesis: that if you ignore things, they will go away. So far I have had excellent results on my ex-girlfriend, ex-friends, and ex-family, but sadly not my body odour. The next set of tests will be on my rent and power bills, and the strange growth on my neck. I'm a little embarrassed by this growth, I guess the shame of the rising weirdness levels remind me of the family chagrin we suffered when my nephew Bartholomew impaled himself on his elbow, in a freak wanking accident.

So anyway, the main focus of practical earth politics lies in the hands of a skinny Maori dude in an indomitable village in Gaul, America, that still resists the Romans, or at least, the *Banco Ambrosiano*.

And what about that band *Dire Straits*, what the fuck is up with them? I listened to their best of and there wasn't a single song about cutting up a corpse and sodomizing all the different bits of the corpse and mashing it all up with a sledgehammer in religious defiance. So come on *Dire Straits*, what is going on here? Are you a brutal slaying grindcore nun-slamming thrash tech-death doomy church-burning black metal band or not?

4

THE REST OF MY FRIDAY NIGHT

When the Prime Minister thought up his new economic strategy, we were bailing out all the way to the bank. Us taxpayers always bail out the banks, I guess taxpayers and money are soon parted. On Friday night I saw Don Brash at a rave – well, it looked like him – *fuck it* I thought, and set him on fire – feel the burn! They didn't bank him though, they wheeled him away on a rather large gurney. I guess a Don Brash raved is a Don Brash gurned.

Roger Douglas disagreed with my financial ideology, my bank account wasn't pretty good. My situation could have been so much better. "Get that bludgy fool who's broke" he said to the policeman who pulled me over while I was pulling a sweet-as wheelie on my beanbag through the ANZ on Featherston St to make a political statement after the policeman chased me, elbow-barged my expired beanbag WOF and suplexed my crappy student wallet, where my ID photo – in denial of my poverty – called me Lord Guyness. "It's pretty funny that you're *totally* broke, your Guyness" the policeman agreed. I explained to him that I lay chained to that financial yoke, no matter how many hours I worked, my bank account trickled down. My bank account always trickles down, I guess a Guyness and debt are soon charted. The cheated friction of a tall Baycorp account phased my wealthless bumrot, worse because I'd saved the last of my rubes up there since that morning. I guess, to throw him off the scent, I had to tell this policeman I had a Don Brash – "hey, smell this" – who was burned.

Listening to politicians argue gave me a headache, felt like the sides of my brain would be soon parted.

"Sir, are your economic views incoherently exposed?" I hoped that they weren't, but off I had dozed, and Don Brash had been burnt. I fell from my bed, no food did I wed, no none would applaud, that I couldn't afford, any two-minute noodles for breakfast-in-mouth, and I'd jockeyed my beanbag until we fled south.

I asked if the bank would take the last of my dignity in exchange for some cash, and they said that they might if I fished it out of the trash. Good thing it was too, for I was money-bereft, but once I cleaned off my dignity there was nothing left!

I wrote WINZ a letter, but Big Brother got me one better, he destroyed all my hope with the thick and the thin of it: "It won't be immediate, it'll be later than most, shove this up your arse, we've just privatised NZ Post."

I wished life was a video game so I could go back to the save point. But I guess a genius and savings are soon parted.

They wanted me to confess my entire financial record. "First could I have an iced tea, and a burrito?" I didn't want to get the answer wrong and go to jail, so I rung up WINZ for some Bill English hook-ups, an extra nine hundred a week. WINZ didn't want anything to do with my torn jeans and scabby knees, my bare feet, my toe jam and my financially burdensome life. I wondered if I could save up the Studylink money and go to Hawaii for a de-stress. But the case manager didn't think so. Pointing at my scrapes and scabs, she said "you've got a rotten knee, maybe you should hide." Then she told me to never do poetry again. I asked her if it was prose correctness gone mad or something, but by that time it was all over. I felt like I was caught in a street with a lot of walls, that were apparently of great importance, but I couldn't climb up any of them. It all reminded me of my uncle Henry who broke his shoulder shaking his own hand too strenuously when he was in deep meditation and finally met himself.

5

SATURDAY NIGHT

I couldn't afford tickets to the Bic Runga gig, so I spent Saturday night home alone looking at a Bic biro. The mosh pit was beyond-metal incredible, just fucking abominably ludicrous. It broke all the windows in our living room and ripped out the ceiling, three walls and a supporting beam in our kitchen. Bits of carpet were mashed all through our food. I'm pretty sure I windmilled so hard while I was headbanging that my hair dried all the clothes on all the washing lines down our street. And I don't think I'll be able to prove it until I hit up my physiology lecturer but I'm convinced my head came off a couple of times in the really groovy intense bits.

Sunday morning joined me in the party. I hadn't planned on having a loud one, but I'd still managed to give myself multiple neck dislocations, an assortment of level thirteen beer-frenzy powerups and hypothalamus inversion. I walked around the apartment gathering up bits of my brain. My mate Baz rang me up and down. "Hey Guy, what are you up to bro?" "Oh yeah, nah, just having a loud one ay bro" I shouted. "There's some really hardcore biros on the Wellington metal scene brah." After the phone got off Baz I began to wonder if I'd been having too many loud ones lately...

You see I just haven't been focussed on the here and now... the other day I was almost run over by a bus because I was thinking about cytosolic protein scaffolding in mammalian cell walls during my walk to the shops... and last week I failed an exam when I accidentally answered an evolutionary genetics question with a twenty-thousand-word essay about crossing the road. I can't seem to think wavy. I can't seem to remember what I'm saying when I'm saying it, so listening to myself talk has become quite entertaining. Sometimes I put a dictaphone with pre-recorded conversations in my throat instead of making up my own blah blah. I just push the play button with a knitting needle through a hole in my neck. That way people know I'm normal.

I've also been very lazy. Instead of going to *Singapore*, I only went to *Talkapore*. I was totally out of balance, and my family and friends chastised me about things I did to excess. Instead of growing a moustache, I grew a ratstache. I clung to mental health by a thread, and tried all sorts of things to mellow out. Instead of going to *Madagascar* I went to *Saneagascar*. I tried to blame my problems on TV and rap music, but my family would have none of it. My mum said I should stop emulating bad people, so instead I began ostrichlating them. I tried taking some panadol, but I accidentally took panateddy.

And on Saturday night, I was in a real mood and I accidentally drove my car up a tree last Saturday! But I'll tell you about that right now, first let me tell you about something else a bit later though.

I've been watching this awesome show with all this massively brutal graphic violence and crimes in it, it's really wicked, you'd enjoy it. It's on at primetime so you don't have to stay up... the soundtrack to it is pretty gay though... it's called *The News*. I guess it's a sort of mockumentary or something. It's really cool cos it's set in the present, like it's happening NOW, and I suppose some of the acting is really amateurish but that's just because they're trying to give it a realistic feel, which makes it even more involving and gripping, like it's scary, like sometimes I think "What if this shit is *REAL*, man?" It'd be really crazy if some of this stuff was actually *HAPPENING TO PEOPLE – I mean what if there WERE thousands of people protesting in Wall Street? What if there really WERE wars killing innocent people? What if good people really WERE the victims of random, drunken violence?* After watching *The News*, I drank ninety-seven tequilas and went into town to start a fight with anyone who looked at me wrong.

Sometimes *The News* is a sad show, there was one episode where all these people died and my mum became quite depressed watching it, she must have been really involved, she watches it every night. You know how people get with drama shows, how they always end up caring heaps about the characters. I don't find it has enough continuity though, they keep changing the characters nearly every episode, but I suppose that is just keeping it racy and fresh. I don't watch every episode, I've got other stuff to focus on at the moment, and I know it's not based on a true story like *Lord of the Rings* is.

To help me relax, and get away from things, I took my new wheels for a spin. What happened was, I was parked up, and then this tree drove into my car! A policeman showed up to help. "Sir, I'm going to need some details." I was so glad to see a friendly officer of the law in his big red truck with all the ladders and hoses to help get me and my custom Celica tow truck down from the tree.

"Where do you live, which province?" said the provinceman. "What are your vitals?" "I'm two kilometres tall and I live a hundred and seventy-eight centimetres away." "Tell us more" he said. I gulped in fear of authority. "I'm four-twenty years old" I continued. "Let me write this down" he said. I gulped in fear of author. "My eye colour is red and my hair is bloodshot."

"Why do you young people have to crash stuff up and waste so much of our time with all this tree-smashing?" the phytologyman asked me. I wanted to explain that society is to blame, it wasn't my fault, I was influenced by other things. Once again I confided in the fuzz-force my emoty-heart-feelingies. You can imagine my pain. There I was in strange old Auckland City lost on a hill, with only one tree on it, that I happened to drive up! I argued: "look at that tree mate, it's parked up there with no lights or handbrake on, right at the top of the hill... don't you think that's a bit dangerous mate? It's an accident waiting to happen! You hit that and your car's chopped in half. I mean, I axe you." He disagreed, and kept pressing me for details. "Hang on mate, are you saying it's perfectly safe to park a tree like that up the top of a hill with no brakes or anchors or anything? Cos if that's safe then I should be allowed to tie all these lawn mowers to my car no problem bro." That's how I was doing four of my community service charges at the same time while I was partying. It felt great to be assertive, without any antagonism or hostility involved. "I'm not telling you how to do your job, but shit mate, are you gonna take that tree's name and address?" They didn't care, but I was persistent, and kept at it: "don't you think we should reshape these trees into something better?" I adzed.

Look, I am being honest here, we have some really psycho trees here in New Zealand! Haven't you seen that *Lord of the Rings* movie where all those trees get a gang together and smash up that old hippy's place? It's like the new level of domestic violence, like *Once Were Warriors* revisited! And they're chucking boulders everywhere, and starting fights hardout! And then those little Scottish dudes swipe all his weed! I think some of our trees might be into drugs and stuff man. I tried to tell the cops the tree I crashed into must have *planted* that stuff they found in my car, but they didn't believe me, they didn't even say lol when I told them trees *plant* things. I guess I didn't want to end up in the jail, lifting weights all day and having spiders tattoo their ink-webs all over my elbows again.

I think because I sometimes get depressed, the police locked me down. "Hey Guy, can you use your Qi Gong superpowers to break us out?" said the boys in lockdown. "Nah, the feds through a way the Qi" I said. "Oh yeah so what do you do for a living now?" they asked.

I told them I was a struggling writer, and how the epic history of my family shenanigans spored me, and had moulded me into a really fun guy. When I told my mum I was going to be a writer all she did was say yes dear yes dear and I was going LET ME FINISH LET ME FINISH because I wasn't FINISHED then I eyedropplered whiskey and Spanish fly onto my keyboard to see if it would make my writing more racy and smashed it with a brick to make my book really hard hitting. It didn't, and I felt failure's embrace again. Beyond Mumderdome has been difficult, two. I was about to speak of my problems but this really arrogant dude said he didn't want to hear it at all, he didn't even care! I felt like a grumpy minotaur on PCP smashing a freshly discharged cowpat with a tennis racket. "What don't you like about my writing?" arh uuuuuuuuuaahh^{h}kCs^{s}sT.

6

HOW TO BE AN EXTREMELY HEALTHY FOOD & FITNESS GURU AND GET ME RICH QUICK SPIRITUALLY

So um totally like totally like yeah nah like um yeah nah true bro so yeah nah mate like totally like um like you know nah yeah like you know like you know like totally so like um like totally like nah yeah bro like totally bit of a nah yeah true bro.

One of the times my great granddude died was when he choked to death on some health food. That's why I wrote this article – so next time he eats some health food, he'll choke back to life. Or maybe not. Maybe he'll just be dead like a normal person - on the toilet, with a fatty bacon sanga layered with extra preservatives and congealing, expired milk coagulant.

I was walking up the hill to university one morning, when I found myself panting and puffing, like totally out of like breath totally. So um like you know? As I sat down for my fifth cigarette break since the bottom of the hill, I began to think about my health. I quickly lit up a second cigarette to help me think, another to help me relax, a fourth for my image, then two more to go with my sunglasses, husky voice, and rockin' mullet.

But I was like beginning to wonder: how long could I survive like totally this? How many times would I be forced to climb this horrible hill, just to learn everything in the world and yell it at everyone at parties on Saturday night? What awful effects was it having on my quality of life, not to mention my bank and cigarette accounts? Why did I keep on running out of cigarettes before I had even got to the top of the hill? *That* is not healthy. Goodness knows university is expensive, but what about the physical toll on us? Can we look up from our purses momentarily to see the unhealthiness of the hill? I had had enough. It was taking my energy, my laziness, the painlessness out of my feet, my sleep, and now my cigarettes. *But what about my health?* How many years was that dumb hill taking from my life? Time I could be spending... uh...

"You'll go far, son" my father said to me when I told him I'd enrolled in universe a T. And I *AM* going far, but that hill is a total bastard, that hill SUCKS. That hill is a *dick*. I need to have SO MANY ciggy breaks to get up there, even when I'm catching the bus! Going the entire way up the hill might be a bit *too* far, like you know? Like totally? Or at least a bit of a totally, right?

I began an internet search to find something that might help me achieve a higher state of life quality and health. I found paydirt: some internet guru's *Get Edgy* program was only $2750, and would not only help me to get healthy, but get business sharp, lose weight, and actually like myself! Which I kind of did already. But apparently I have all these huge problems in my life that I wasn't even aware of! Like apparently modern life is really stressful! This website reckons I'm stressed! I didn't know that! I suppose it's a good thing I found out though. This guru has thoughtfully created the *Get Edgy* program for people like me, who have all these stupid big hills in the way of their life goal of not walking up any hills. I also need to get lots of money so I can give it to this internet guru so he can teach me how to get rich quick!

According to my guru, a big part of being healthy has, surprisingly, a lot to do with what you put in your body. I didn't expect that! He says you should use a lot of these weird objects of possible extra-planetary origin called 'vegetables' that don't look anything like actual food. They're obviously for decorative purposes only; for helping with self-esteem when posh friends come over. He also recommends a rather bizarre form of torture known to internet-phobes as 'exercise', which looks like some type of military combative art, I guess you could possibly use it on people who propose building lecture theatres on hills.

I was about to do some of these 'exercises', but I don't think my chi is quite ready for that, and it's really hard to do push-ups with a ciggy in my hand. So I think I should bulk a little, do a little carb-loading, you know? So I'll start dinner with parched pheasant soaked in jellied yak hoof a la pineapple marinade, scented grouse liver pudding with cloves floating in a raw, unfermented guinness broth with sheep brains and horse meat sundae with grated pig tusk shavings for dessert. And some baboon meat. It's okay to indulge once in a while, right? Of course it is! So I'm eating heaps, because I like myself! I'm okay with my body! It looks like you could still do with losing a bit of weight though, I think. You're obviously not smoking enough. I'll just have a bite of this crème brûlée with golden lemon marzipan, a plate or two of these deep-fried strawberries filleted with quaint village innkeeper's gruel and the yolk of tiger beetle and Australian lizard eggs on a chateau '68 sauce with monkey breast dumplings and lashings of wild hornet honey from the mountains of Uzbekistan, and the biley milk squeezed from the supple teat of an amiable grandmother hippo, mellowed in monsoon season.

Here, you can have a lettuce leaf; I don't think I'll be eating much of that. I mean why's it all *green?* Yuk. And just "what" on earth is *this* thing? A "carrot"? It's fucking ORANGE, dude. I'm not eating that, it's probably radioactive if it's bright *orange.* It's just about glowing! Trust me, I'm a scientist. That's one of those 'foods' that grows in the ground, right? Oooo... that's kind of... sick... that's almost creepy... you can go for it, I might try a wee nibble if you're alive in the morning. I'm not giving you any of my carb dinner though, I would, but I've only really got enough for myself.

Now it's time to look at food groups. The best food groups are Meat Loaf, Bread, Cream, Bananarama, Pearl Jam and The Spice Girls. Actually nah, those food groups are all sellouts. Too commercial for me, too mainstream. I like more alternative food groups.

My favourite bestest food groups are KFC, death metal, red, and chips. Chips are given at most good dining establishments. Red is in tomato sauce, most pizzas, chewing gum, cookies, lollies, strawberry shortcake and pie. KFC is down the road and alcohol is right here. No! You can't have *any* of mine. Man, I'm *so* sick of people trying to scam me out of my drinks... oooooooohhhhhhh... ... can I have some of yours? Just give me a bit... just... can you give me a third ... ... actually round it up to half, that's a bit fairer.

So we see where nutrition fits into the scream of things. Just make sure you don't eat the wrong food. Eating the wrong food can lead to people harassing you, being underweight and overheight, wasting all your money on health books, and death. And apparently being dead is not good for you at all. If you are dead, you should see a doctor.

Actually... forget about doctors... why don't you try some of these wicked dietary supplements I have? I've lost so much wait since I started taking this WICKED new dietary supplement called heron, or hero, or something, that stuff is SO good at helping with weight loss. Now I'm down to a healthy thirty-nine kilos! That is pretty slim for a 32-year old man, right? I think you should definitely start taking it, especially if you have an addictive personality - just to help you chill out, you know? Help you to relax, man. And you only need a teaspoon a day!

So if I'm doing all this health food, with all of these hero and baccy supplements why do I feel so unfit and lazy? ... Ah, who gives a shit? But tobacco apparently is a powerful herb used by the Navajo and Sioux tribes in their medicine. I have been using this wicked stuff from the Rothmans and Pall Mall tribes. It's good to get back to nature and away from all the corporations.

I'm grateful you've looked at these issues with me. They are, in most societies, a big deal. After all, I've read that at least eight out of every ten people eventually die of something. When I wrote to the government about this aspect of modern life, and just what they were planning to do about it... let's just say I was *not* impressed with the haste of their reply, in spite of my nagging. Anyway, thanks for your offer of some yummy muesli, but I usually go against the grain.

7

HOW TO COPE WITH WRITER'S BLOCK

8

INTERVENTION

A few of my parents, siblings and close friends all came into my room today. They looked very seriously at me, their mood somber and sad, perhaps a tad fearful... it was honestly very hard to tell. That was partly because I wasn't paying any attention to them, I was reading this amazing touching book about this totally weird guy who had kind of failed in life, you know, barely ever held down a job, wasted all his money on stupid stuff, and turned to drinking because of his low self-esteem. I have honestly no idea why I connected so much with it. But he had a lot of *energy*, you know? He had *passion*, and if he would just *discipline himself*, and channel that passion into something beautiful - if he could just quit all the bad habits, he could do great things! But he just wanted to sit around and play video games all day, drink bland cheap student beer, and waste his life on flavourless pursuits. His parents and siblings had just come into his room all serious-like, as if they wanted to save him from his own stupid behaviour and it sounded like they were going to tell him something *REALLY IMPORTANT AND SINCERE*. But he was just sitting there reading a book or something, and wasn't even listening to them. So I was sort of laughing at this dude, he didn't have his stuff together, was really lazy and clueless, spaced out all the time, never doing anything awesome like me. I was thinking 'mate, you dick' and all this, cos he was just going nowhere fast, not like me, I'm at a university! Well, I'm not there now, I haven't been today. I'll go tomorrow.

My mother pulled up the park bench next to my bed. "Look Guy" she said. "It's time you got all your problems and your bad jobless pungent self-destructive habits under control. I mean you're thirty and a half and still at university but you're not working hard enough. Your family is intervening, and we just want what's best for you, but you need some discipline in your life."

But when she said that, I was all of a sudden busy being asleep! Then I was lolling because she said "hard enough"! Wow, man! Then my brother spoke up: "Dude, we're having an intervention... for you. We do care about you, and we think you're doing some very self-destructive things at the moment... if you had a job, you'd be much better off... we want you to change... we've planned this intervention for you..."

Wow, an intervention! Sweet! "Yeah, nah, sweet as" I said. "I'll just do this briefcase of uppers and caffeine and listen to all of my *Def Leppard* and *Manowar* albums and stay up for three days straight, you know?"

Then I'd be ready for an intervention! Power metal and headbanging to some live *Decapitated* would totally psych me up for it, you know? And I could get the VIBE of it, and really get a hundred and ten percent *into* it! That way I'd be AWAKE enough to HANDLE it and SEE if I could, you know, then I could POWER into the intervention, paying attention to it! And make it the best, most greatest, most bestest ultimatest intervention ever!

But wait! ... This is where my story gets scary... they all wanted me...
to do the intervention sober!

And like all sober decisions, it turned out to be a bad one. I didn't
wake up in a weird place with puke everywhere. I didn't wake up in bed
with a really gross ugly croney older woman. I didn't put wheels on a
snooker table and ride it off my roof. I didn't go to a wicked-ass death
metal gig and get stabbed in the pancreas.

After the intervention I bought a car. People told me to get the
car I need, not show off and get something unnecessarily flashy. I got a
Porsche. I needed a Porsche so I could show everyone that I could afford
to buy Porsches on random whims whenever I felt like it. As soon as I
paid for the Porsche I declared bankruptcy. Then I drank two hundred
and zero beers. *That's almost two hundred and something beers!* Then this
idiot crashed his tree into my Porsche!

I pulled up the venetian blinds and opened the French doors I had
specially fitted to my Porsche. I walked out onto the wooden balcony
I'd made for it and just about threw the barbeque and one of my
beer fridges at this douchebag. "OI MATE!" I screamed. "MOVE YA
BLOODY TREE OUTTA THE WAY! I'M TRYING TO DRIVE MY
PORSCHE THROUGH HERE!" I couldn't believe all the cool people
hanging out in the forest were seeing my awesome Porsche being cut off
by some boy racer's lame birch tree. It reminded me of the sudden demise
of my hyperactive but very underweight friend Percy, who died when he
accidentally flung himself out the window of an aeroplane toilet in an
out of control, high-speed eyebrow-trimming calamity.

I was pretty keen to ram this guy who cut me off, but I walked away because I didn't want to have to take my Porsche to the arborist AGAIN. The last time it got damaged was still fresh in my mind, and I didn't want to have to repeat the incredible ordeal of getting some new bark fitted on the doors, and send away to Europe for some overpriced root xylem for the engine hydraulics, deep in the concrete piles of the porsche.

I was just glad I wasn't out in my pohutakawa, that one has a dodgy clutch, and the handbrake on it is fucked. And the City Council keep on denying my requests to raise the height of all the power lines in the city, so the top branches always snag on them.

9

HOW TO BE THE BEST WORLD IN THE WRITER

So you want to be a writer? It is indeed a noble occupation to occupate. Obviously, if you are going to do something, it is worth doing to *absolute and TOTAL PERFECTION.* That's why I wrote this article... which I guess is OK. (Actually, I think it kind of sucks.)

Look mate: let me tell you something about writing. It's hard. And it's pretty boring. Hardly anyone has any attention span these days! Lots of people try to make life exciting with bungy jumping and all sorts of extreme sports, so good luck trying to impress all the pompous elite cool people with a crummy BOOK.

What is so great about books? Well, you can leave them round your house so friends will think that you know how to read. That is one use for them. Now, if you're going to be a writer you want good reviews, don't you? Not arty - farty, ambiguous things like "Magnificent, compelling" – that is crap. You don't want this one either: "A must - read for anyone in the field of hyperterrestrial ornithology" - no, you want tyre-burning flame-spitting shirt-ripping damsel-saving passionate reviews.

And if you can't be bothered writing quality, just write really offensive drivel, just pick an extreme viewpoint on a controversial topic and it will sell HEAPS just because people are desensitized WHICH IS WHY YOU HAVE TO ALWAYS WRITE IN CAPITALS TO BE INTELLIGENT, but put someone else's name on it so you don't get in trouble. Like ages ago I wrote this thing called *The Satanic Verses* and just made up this random foreign sounding name for the pseudonym. I don't think many people were too worried about it though. So that was cool. Anyway, I'm glad it didn't last long, and I do this thing instead, working for you. It's a pretty sweet gig. You're not like a total fascist boss or anything.

So, reviews. You want reviews like "This book made me want to blow up a toilet and shoot dried cowpats out of a tank at an old folks' home" and "This book made me want to urinate off the tallest building in the city." These two are especially good reviews. Incidentally, when I first showed this column to the editor of our university magazine, he sprinted up to the roof of our four-story office and urinated right on some first-years, who looked like they were used to it (I think one of them even opened his mouth a bit as if he liked it).

To get reviews like these cool ones you need some ideas, man, and not that silly politically correct crap that dominates the best-seller lists worldwide. No, you need to be true to your heart, gutsy, brave, a fearless literary warrior, like King Stephen, when he pulled his mighty space bar out of stone, imbued with his sacred typewriter of redemption and purification. But you also need energy and some cosmic stuff going on, like out of space stuff, imagination. So when do people get their best ideas and remain true to themselves?

You know those rare times where you go to a party and before the party is in full swing and everyone is sober and hasn't loosened up because they're nervous about all the people they don't know and they don't want to say hi to anyone or make eye contact? And then one *really* drunk person comes along and makes a dick of themselves by saying what everyone is thinking? And doing really funny cool stuff like telling the well-dressed people in suits how much they'd *hate* to have an office job? Well, to be a really top of the line writer - and you can trust me - you need to be like the drunkest person at the party <hic>. I mean, be true to your heart or something, that's what I mean, I don't mean get a drinking problem. Just do whatever I sway, I mean say, but you're still responsible.

So getting the balance here is very important, and in all sincere seriousness - just pretend I'm leaning my whole body weight on your shoulder breathing right into your face and burping; telling you that there's so many hot people at this party, but they're probably all way too cool for me, I'm rough round the edges you know, I'm not a mainstream person, and I'm shaking your hand and going "so are we good?" again and again and again and asking your name and saying sorry for being drunk and then shaking your hand again and again and asking you if I shook your hand yet and getting your name wrong and saying that you probably don't like me coming up to you, and I've actually forgotten what I was talking about after the last time I got your name wrong, but whatever the hell I *was* talking about, I WAS - *RIGHT* - AND THE OTHER PERSON WAS - *WRONG* - AND THAT'S THE - *END* - OF THE DISCUSSION -

Sorry, I'll start that paragraph again. You see what I mean about balance, though, right? I hope you do, because I think there you put me off or something. But getting really into it will separate you from the "magnificent, compelling" lot. This "balance" is a technique that serious writers like Stephen King and John Grisham use very well.

Stephen King of course, deserves a mention here. This man has written a colossal amount of very high quality material. No other author, except perhaps The Internet, has written as much as King. His first novel, *Cartie*, was a horror story about a demonic go-kart that wasn't warranted or registered and kept getting pulled over and fined by police. It ended with some horrifying passive-aggressive customer service clerks at *Wellington Parking and Infringement Services*, and a few nasty letters to some very scared editors. This was followed by a string of bestsellers, among them *Misery*, about the declining quality of *Shortland Street*; *Twit*, a novel about this really annoying clown in a dairy, the massive epic *1408 Chapters*, and an all work and no play hands on breaking and entering guide for alcoholics, called *The Shimmying*.

There is also *Night Shift*, about a gas station worker who drinks too many energy drinks and can't sleep through his shift like he normally does. As well as these, King has penned *Gerald's Game*, which is about a really unfair Dungeon Master who won't let any adventuring party have more than one wizard, and *Four Past Midnight* – a terrifying, frustrating and sadistic tale about a man who misses the last Saturday train to Upper Hutt and has to sleep at the bus stop outside Maccas.

King has also had movies made of his work, like *The Running Man* which is about an actor with a cool accent who is always getting chased and attacked for saying cheesy one-liners, but he *NEVER* seems to learn. It's a testament to King's amazing storytelling, and the intense realism and power of the characters he creates, that the story is powerful enough to go so far as to break the fourth wall and this actor keeps using cheesy one-liners *in subsequent movies*. Another is *The Mist*, which is about some government-level stoners that somehow hotbox the whole planet. King is also the creator of *The Dark Half*, a movie about a bogan dude in Porirua who can't be bothered getting a job, and the critically acclaimed *The Foreshore Bank Retention*. This is a compelling, magnificent story about a really abusive boy racer who just about beats up his Mrs and goes to jail. There, he meets Morgan Freeman, a dude from Stokes Valley with the mean hook-ups, who shows him boy racing is just wrong in principle, on every level. Eventually he aids in the escape of the protagonist, who goes to live in the Marlborough Sounds and starts a dope plot in the bush. The movie ends tearfully on the beach with the ex-boy racer dude character trying to buy a fifty bag, but saying he can't pay for it until Wednesday when his dole goes in and Freeman is wondering whether he should let the bro tick or not. Naturally, King is on the beers quite a bit to come up with these great ideas for novels.

King's scariest: his guide to writing, and memoirs – *On Writing*. It is utterly uncompromising in its fear, especially when he tells you to have a good work ethic and be disciplined in your approach to it, wow that bit is just TERRIFYING! He says you should write six hours a day! And then he talks about giving up beer! *AAAAAAAAAIIIIIIEEEEE!!!!* When I read that I was just shitting myself! I had to put it down after reading that bit. Sorry, but I couldn't finish that book, it was getting too scary for me. I guess that's why he is the master.

King's wife, Dean Koontz, is also a best-selling novelist. Their six children and pet canary are all best-selling novelists too.

John Irving is another great writer whose books you should read instead of wasting all your time on facebook like a normal person. Irving has penned many books, among them *The World According to Crap,* which is the story of a really unfunny comedian who can't stop telling these lame jokes all the time, even during normal conversations, like someone asking what time it is ("time to get a watch" for example), and *Family Guy* is always taking the piss. It has a cool ending where everyone dies. Actually, it's probably easier to not bother with being a writer. You might as well flag. Just give up, like this.

10

SECOND TO LAST THINGY/
OUTRODUCTION

I guess none of us know exactly when this life of ours will, or will never, end. So I just want to say thanks for reading my book and wish you well for the rest of eternity or ten minutes or whatever. And whether you follow Richard Dawkins or Jesus, or whether you *lead* Richard Dawkins or Jesus, it makes no difference to me. I still think you're silly. I think you're droopy old lady boobs dangling into a hat full of poo.

It is, I guess, all a matter of degree. Have you got a degree? Oh no, *YOU* don't, only *I* have... so... I guess I must be right. Well, OK actually, to be scientifically precise, I haven't got a degree gotten YET, but I'll get it one day. Nah... yeah, I'll get it later. Maybe I'll get it tomorrow or something.

But I'm not just theoretically a educated person. I've also had a experience. In this experience, I was watching TV, watching this dude have an actual *experience*, going "far out mean one bro" not just in a lecture theatre watching someone else *talk* about a book someone had written about someone else's experience, but I was *actually watching* this dude have his experience on TV! It's amazing what you can learn from skipping lectures to stay home and watch TV.

Not all of these experiences have been weird or bizarre. Some of them have been down and to the right strange. Let me tell you about this really trippy psychedelic experience I had the other day: I was looking up, and there was this thing above me... this glowing orb of light... with an amazing circular structure around it. What the hell was it? Was it a UFO? This thing was totally still and it shone bright, infatuating light onto and all around me, engaging me in its hypnotic glare. It was extremely beautiful, amazing and intense, the massive rays of light bro shining on me coming from a central infinite oroborous, I was *awash* in this incredible cosmic light. What was it? I couldn't look away, I became totally unaware of the rest of my environment. It bathed me, coated me with incandescence, and I lost all track of time and space, my eyes toing and froing into and out of focus, sending billions of these strange photonic messages to my brain. WAS I FINALLY CONTACTING ALIEN BEINGS? Their light was welcoming and warm, they had heard me! *They had seen the smoke signals from my bongs!* ***HAD COSMIC ALIEN BEINGS TRAVELLED THE UNFATHOMABLE EXPANSES OF THE UNIVERSITY JUST TO TALK TO ME?*** Wow! I stayed like that for about an hour, I was frozen, like a headlight being stuck in a freezer by a deer.

So there I was, underneath this incredible sphere, just buzzing and buzzing and buzzing, wondering what it was.

Then I realised I was just lying on the floor with the light on. Again. It wasn't aliens, it was just my bedroom light. I'd woken up, so I tried to go back to sleep. But the people in my brain were just laughing at me for ages about it, they just wouldn't stop poking fun at me. It was a powerful learning experience.

It saddens me to say I will be leaving you soon. I've told you a bit about my life and I wouldn't want to overdo it. Instead of an epilogue for you, I have got a man I met at university to write a sort of goodbye. Just between you and me he is a bit of a dick. I think it's because his parents spoiled him. They wrapped him in cotton wool, instead of cotton denim like a normal kid. Or denim wool or whatever. I went to his enormous house and just looking at it made me tired, I wouldn't want to walk around all those staircases all day, so I just passed out on the carpet.

Then these butlers turned up out of nowhere and one of them had a bowl and a towel, and all this soap, and started washing my jacket with window cleaner or something, and I had to say "mate, I almost got Alex from *Cannibal Corpse* to sign this jacket, that's why it hasn't been cleaned, and the stain is where that fulla's head came off at the *Ulcerate* gig, all that blood is a memory, mate that's nostalgia right there." At first I thought they didn't understand sentimentality. But someone told me these things are actually matters of class. I thought about it, and wondered what I could do to change things. It was true that there were class problems and possibly unfair situations in the world. For instance, the university faculty had structured my timetable so that most of my classes were in the morning, which meant I was attending them tired, asleep, hungover or still partying. New Zealand had become so ridiculously bureaucratic I was not allowed to just wheel my bed into the lecture theatre for the semester and learn the lecture via sleep-induction. This having to get up early all the time *definitely* felt in some ways unfair, as if some invisible hand had merchanted and manufactured the promised student sleep-in away.

Anyway, I will leave you now with a "later class" gentleman who I believe will explain this invisible handicap. This man is the son of Lord Bonkington, or some other politician, which is pretty hardout, and he said if I let him get an article for his political science paper into my book, so my morning class mates could see it, and understand his point of view he would let me ride round in his helicopter! Sweet, huh?

So off I go now, I'm outta here, I'm on my bike, I'm going, without saying bye, without waving, without even txting L8R, because this dude is doing it for me. And I all lived happily ever after. And people with depression didn't.

11

WAR ON THE LOWER CLASS

A discourse from His Dukeness Bramtonley Archibaldcroftbarrington-ford Albertson-Smythe Wuthering Farty-Tossle Franciburn Barnard Sir Willoughby Archlord Junior III of Honey-In-Porridge Manor, four pubs east of the town of Splatterypoo, during tea time after a rather most splendid game of lawn bowls on the twelfth green of the verdure, that was quite a dashingly spot of neck-and-neck for a minute there.

<u>The Discourse Reads Thus:</u>

Ladies and gentlemen: I am simply a normal man, in a normal life, just like you. I am not special or privileged. Nor am I deprived of the knowledge and experience of - quote unquote, as they say - the real world - and by that I mean doing things, hands on, for, and by, comma, myself. As I stand here with my gardener, my butler, my haberdasher, my clothes washing maid, my clothes drying maid, my clothes folding maid, my wardrobe door opening maid, my clothes putting away maid, my wardrobe door closing maid, our family pastry chef, our vegetable chef, our exotic vegetable chef, our chutney, jam, and marmalade chef, our cup of tea chef, our South Park chef, our family of ethnically different servants, my fox-hunting dogs, mother, grandmother, and Prince William Featherybollocks Ponce-Bucket of Bouncy Castle, I address you, the common man or woman, as you have your butler read this to you, no doubt over truffles, badger-tongue stew, goose-feet marmalade, and most delightful lashings of Humphrington's Tea, obviously only to be had with fresh cream whipped at a whipping post from a freshly whipped organically grown cow, with minimal skin pigmentation, that had been quite obviously taught from a young age to never lactate in public.

As I have declared, I am no different to any of you other students enlisted in university education. I have a pool-side sixteen-acre mansion with eighty bedrooms, five dining rooms, and a drawing room complete with snooker tables and indoor life-size cricket ground, all of which I will own when father passes; a European antique Alfa Romeo car collection, tennis courts, squash courts, high and supreme courts, silica quartz, a botanical hideaway deep within my rather modest outdoor coin collection of two acres by four acres, and a seat in the pews at parliament. I also have solid gold urinals in all nine hundred and two bathroom ensuites. As Phil Ken Sebben would say, "There's nothing like gold on gold!"

When Pater took me to university this afternoon for etiquette club and a *rather* spiffing quantum poetry lecture, we had the usual tussles with traffic finding a place to park our helicopter, and a strange creature with thickened matted ropey hairlets impolitely accosted me for tobacco, using the quite uncivil incongruance "bro". So you see, I suffer muchly. Yesterday, while playing Brahms' *Minuet Sonata in G# Minor* on the pianoforte, I almost sneezed! Mother said it was *dreadfully* vulgar.

One day we had to take the Mercedes Benz to University! Well, we were *awfully* embarrassed about taking one of our cheaper cars in, but there you go, sacrifices and such, I'm sure you understand. It was a shocking blow to the family name, all the chaps at dressage that week ending were having a jolly old rum go at us – no rotting, I dare say! The cheeking-ness of voluminous slanders! I'm just glad they know I had my butler write all my essays for me last year! Like I say, sacrifices must be made. But these business class fingertips weren't made like the common man's! I'm not holding one of those revolting "biro" calligraphers! And imagine the germs on those shared computer keyboards! I'll jab a serving wench until she shudders at the thought!

This philistinism brings me to the topic at hand: Simply do your duty to Queen and Country, pay your taxes like good honest citizens, and stop these pandering protests. And get a job while you're at it! Don't go accepting these government handouts! Stop these marches and such, with your placards and slogans, and go to work! Don't worry about old politics, that's *our* game. Why, let the upper classes do the thinking!

Now recently I was at this Cuba Carnival, rattling my jewellery and gadding about, having a bally old show of a hoot, when I saw rather a lot of people jumping about like a bunch of monkeys, with not much clothing on at all! Spoils the mood, a tad, methinks. 'Dancing' they call it! Rubbish! Do they even understand music theory? Let me tell you something about dancing: The man puts one arm above the woman's corseted hips, they endure a gracious introduction, she curtsies to him quaintly, and once they've sloshed back some Merlot '73, met their respective parents, *and* if it's deduced they have similar amounts in the bank, they must be just right for each other, especially if they're cousins.

Send the sods off on a big expensive honeymoon with taxpayer money, say I, and let them figure it out for themselves! We certainly want none of this 'sex education' pornography in the classroom of all places! Putting balloons on bananas, and all that tosh! What's that got to do with anything?

Now I went on one date with a young lady, and I thought I heard a gassy turbulence emitting from her behind – filthy! And then she laughed! I dare say! I would have turned my nostrils upward, but I was worried my breathing might be compromised. I had one of my butlers quickly slap her taxi driver's face, call her a bounder, a cad, and a mountebank! Thenasfar, towhich, bespeckled withon, towhit, we left – *and with narry a look back I say!* When I told father about the whole thing over pilchard caviar and pheasant larynx that night, he was *rather* miffed. Certainly, a daughter of common gentry.

Well, that's about all from me, I'm sure you've learned a thing or two about the harsh *plight of man*, dare say I. I'm off to have a Gerald Lord Sandwich – it's a fantastic idea – you get this "flour" out of grains, heat it, make a "loaf", which is then marginalised in twain cleftings by a group of butlers, with some edible or other betwixt. I'm having a delicious albatross-beak puree, swine foie gras, vole-nose pickle and aardvark tail paté fricassee upon the inner side of mine.

Signing off,
With glorious sunlight shining out from between my clenched buttocks,
*Lord Bramtonley, et cetera., et. Al., ad infinitum, ad nauseum, *,8,1.*